Jacqueline Woodson

by Julie Murray

Abdo
CHILDREN'S AUTHORS
Kids

Abdo Kids Jumbo is an Imprint of Abdo Kids
abdobooks.com

abdobooks.com

Published by Abdo Kids, a division of ABDO, P.O. Box 398166, Minneapolis, Minnesota 55439.

Printed in the United States of America, North Mankato, Minnesota.

102021

012022

THIS BOOK CONTAINS RECYCLED MATERIALS

Photo Credits: Alamy, Getty Images, iStock, Shutterstock PREMIER, ©TED Conference p11 / CC BY-NC-ND 2.0

Production Contributors: Teddy Borth, Jennie Forsberg, Grace Hansen
Design Contributors: Candice Keimig, Pakou Moua

Library of Congress Control Number: 2020948014

Publisher's Cataloging-in-Publication Data

Names: Murray, Julie, author.

Title: Jacqueline Woodson / by Julie Murray

Description: Minneapolis, Minnesota : Abdo Kids, 2022 | Series: Children's authors | Includes online resources and index.

Identifiers: ISBN 9781098207229 (lib. bdg.) | ISBN 9781098208066 (ebook) | ISBN 9781098208486 (Read-to-Me ebook)

Subjects: LCSH: Woodson, Jacqueline--Juvenile literature. | Authors--Biography--Juvenile literature. | Children's books--Juvenile literature.

Classification: DDC 809.8928--dc23

Table of Contents

Early Life 4

Books 10

Legacy 20

Timeline 22

Glossary 23

Index 24

Abdo Kids Code 24

Early Life

Jacqueline Woodson was born on February 12, 1963, in Columbus, Ohio. Her family moved to South Carolina and then to Brooklyn, New York.

Brooklyn, NY
Columbus, OH
Greenville, SC

Jacqueline loved to read, write, and tell stories. Her fifth-grade teacher told her that she was a good writer. This **inspired** her!

Stained Glass
brown girl dreaming

Jacqueline graduated from college with a degree in English. Later, she took a children's book writing class. There, an editor heard readings from her stories. This led to Woodson's first book deal.

ANOTHER
BROOKLYN
A NOVEL
JACQUELINE

Books

Young readers can relate to Jacqueline's stories. Her topics include race, **class**, and family. Many of her books have a connection to people and places in her life.

TED

Last Summer with Maizon was Woodson's first book. It was published in 1990. It is a **novel** about a young girl dealing with loss and hard changes in her life.

Miracle's Boys is a young adult **novel** about three brothers from Harlem. They help each other after the deaths of their parents.

After Tupac and D Foster
miracle's boys
miracle's boys
"THREE-TIME"
Newbery Honor Author
JACQUELINE
WOODSON
JACQUELINE WOODSON
JACQUELINE WOODSON
miracle's boys
miracle's boys
miracle's boys

The Other Side is a children's picture book about two young neighbors. One is Black and the other is white. The two learn that a fence can't keep a friendship from forming.

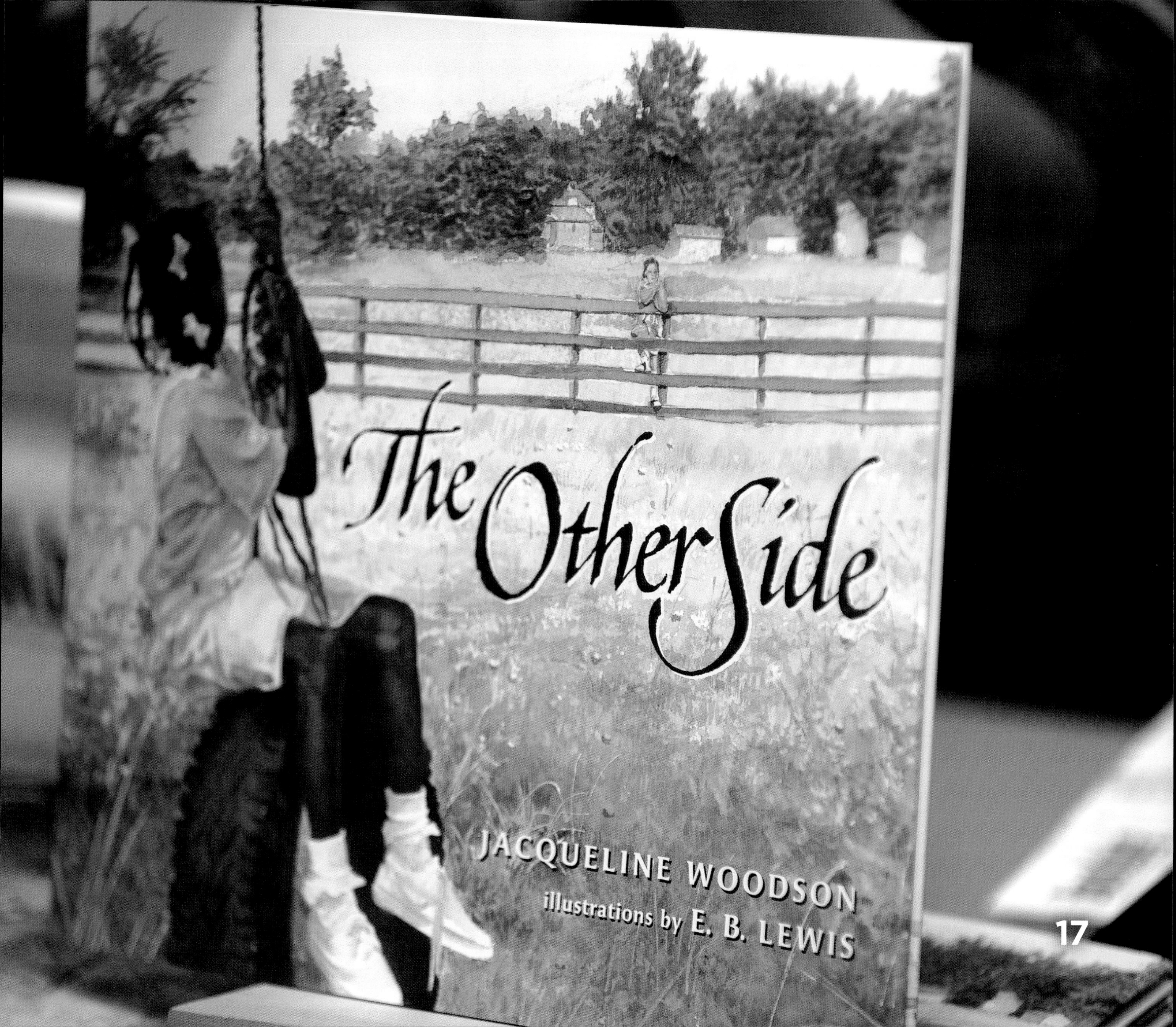
The Other Side
JACQUELINE WOODSON
illustrations by E. B. LEWIS

Brown Girl Dreaming is a **memoir** written in **free verse**. It is about growing up during the 1960s and ’70s. The memoir discusses **racism** and identity.

National Book
Foundation
National Book
Foundation
National Book
Foundation
brown girl dreaming
NATIONAL BOOK AWARD
WINNER
National Book

Legacy

Jacqueline has written more than 40 books for children, teens, and young adults. She has won many awards for her writing. Today, she lives in Brooklyn, New York, with her partner and their two children.

National
Book
Awards
National
Book
Awards

Timeline

1963 — **February 12** Jacqueline Woodson is born in Columbus, Ohio.

1985 — Jacqueline graduates from Adelphi University.

1990 — Woodson's first book, *Last Summer with Maizon* is published.

2000 — *Miracle's Boys* is published.

2001 — *The Other Side* is published.

2005 — *Miracle's Boys* is made into a TV miniseries.

2006 — Woodson is awarded her first John Newbery Medal.

2014 — *Brown Girl Dreaming* is published.

2014 — Woodson wins the National Book Award for Young People's Literature.

2020 — Woodson is awarded the McArthur Fellowship.

Glossary

class – a group of people who have a similar way of life and position in society.

free verse – poetry that does not rhyme or have a regular rhythm.

inspired – filled with the urge or ability to feel or do something, especially to do something creative.

memoir – an account of the author's own experiences and life.

novel – a longer work of fiction, usually having a plot and characters.

racism – unfair treatment of people based on the opinion that one race is better than another race or races.

Index

awards 20

birth 4

Brown Girl Dreaming 18

career 8, 20

education 6, 8

family 4, 20

Last Summer with Maizon 12

Miracle's Boys 14

New York 4, 14, 20

Ohio 4

Other Side, The 16

South Carolina 4

works 10, 12, 14, 16, 18, 20